Don't Wake the Bear!

For Andy, who sometimes wakes up grumpy
(but mostly lets her sleep) – S.S.

For Phils … play on – C.P.

First published in Great Britain in 2010 by Little Tiger Press, an imprint
of Magi Publications.

ISBN 978-0-545-69576-3

12 11 10 9 8 7 6 5 4 3 2 1   14 15 16 17 18 19/0

Printed in the U.S.A.   40

First Scholastic paperback printing, February 2014

Don't Wake the Bear!

Steve Smallman

Caroline Pedler

SCHOLASTIC INC.

It was Spring Party Day, the best day of the year,
so why were the animals trembling with fear?
They'd heard growling noises and crept up to see...
A huge bear asleep in the old hollow tree!

SPRING PARTY **TODAY** at the old hollow tree

"Oh, no!" they all cried. "But our party's today!
How can we get ready with **him** in the way?"
"**I'll wake him up!**" cried a little brown hare.
"No, no," they all whispered. "Please, don't wake the bear!"

"Bears," Badger said, "are **enormous** and **hairy**.
If you wake them up, they get angry and **scary!**
We'll **still** have our party, though, if we take care.
Be quiet as mice so we **don't** wake the bear!"

So they tippy-toed off without making a peep,
to get party things while the bear was asleep.
And the ants carried **wibbling**, wobbling stacks
of **dishes** and saucers and cups on their backs.

Badger brought in a huge, yummy dessert,
then he tripped, and it fell with a **splat** in the dirt!

zz z z z grr humph z z z zz

The bear stretched and grumbled, which gave them a scare.
"Shh!" they all whispered. "Please, don't wake the bear!"

The lanterns were **carefully** hung in the trees.
The **mice tied up** ribbons that danced on the **breeze**.
They brought in the very last **blueberry tart**,
and **their party** was now almost ready to **start!**

Then Hare cried, "There's only one thing left to do!"
And he grabbed a **balloon** and he blew and he blew,

and he **blew** and he **blew** till the others cried, "STOP! If it gets any **bigger**, it's going to—"

The bear **stretched** and **groaned** and they all held their breath.
Then his eyes **flickered** open and scared them to death!
"**Run**, run and hide!" they all cried in despair.
"Now we're in trouble—we've **woken the bear!**"

"WHO DARES WAKE ME UP?" growled the bear angrily.

Hare said in a small, shaky voice.

"It was me!

Our party is going to start very **soon**.

I was trying to **help**, but I popped my balloon...".

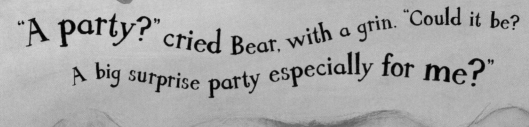

"A party?" cried Bear, with a grin. "Could it be?
A big surprise party especially for me?"

"Oh, **thank you** for waking me up, little bunny.
I'll come to your party and bring you some **honey!**"

And even though Bear was enormous and hairy,
they found he was great **fun** and not a bit scary.
He danced and he partied with everyone there,
and they all cheered, "Hurray for our new **friend**, the bear!"